Words to my future daughter

Parinita Sharma

BlueRoseONE.com
Stories Matter
NewDelhi • London

BLUEROSE PUBLISHERS
India | U.K.

BlueRose ONE
Stories Matter
NewDelhi • London

For permissions requests or inquiries regarding this publication, please contact:

BLUEROSE PUBLISHERS
www.BlueRoseONE.com
info@bluerosepublishers.com
+91 8882 898 898
+4407342408967

ISBN: 978-93-7310-318-1

Cover Design: Aman Sharma
Typesetting: Manisha Rawat

First Edition: October 2025

DEDICATION:

"To the daughter I dream of,

and to every girl who has ever needed to hear these words"

For the girl I once was, and for the girl who will one day call me "Mumma."

From a daughter who has learned life's lessons, and now shares them with you – my next me.

MAY THESE WORDS GUIDE, COMFORT AND INSPIRE YOU.

OPENING NOTE:

"My dearest future daughter,

Your Mumma doesn't know your name yet, or the sound of your laughter, or the colour of your eyes, not even your hair colour. But I already know one thing with certainty—you are deeply loved and always be close to my heart. This book is my gift to you. These are the words I wish someone had whispered to me when I was younger, the lessons I am still learning, and the truths I carry in my heart are only shared to you because you are the next me, I never want you to feel left out whenever the world turns around.

One day, when you hold this book, I hope it feels like holding my hand. Whenever you feel lost, broken, or unsure, open these pages and hear me speaking to you. Because no matter the distance, no matter the time, you will never be alone. Your Mumma is always by your side to support you in whenever you feel alone."

ACKNOWLEDGEMENT:

First and foremost, with folded hands, I bow to **Mahadev**, whose blessings guide me in every step of my journey and whose presence gives me the strength to dream and to write.

(OM NAMAH PARVATI PATAH HAR HAR MAHADEV)

I am deeply grateful to my **parents**, the roots of my existence.

To my maa – *for the gift of life,* for raising me with love, and for showing me the beauty of being a daughter.

To my papa – *for shaping me into a queen,* for his unwavering strength, and for believing in me always.

To my friends, **Teesta, Kritika and Harshita (author of 'A SOUL IN CHAINS')** who have stood by me in little and big ways, encouraging me to trust my words and share my heart – thank you for walking beside me.

To the one, whose name remains unspoken yet whose presence gave me the hope of being a good mother for my future daughter – thank you for encouraging me through all ups and downs.

I owe this vision, which blossomed into the very soul of this book.

"It is their love, guidance, and belief in me that allows these words to reach you today."

This book exists because of all of you — each of you a chapter of my heart.

CONTENTS

ON LOVE

My dear daughter,

One day you will ask me, ***"MUMMA, what does love truly mean?"***

And that day I will tell you,

"Love, my dear, is not just a word. It may be made of four small letters, but it carries within it a universe of responsibilities."

Love is not just a feeling; it is a language of the soul.

It is the silent bond that connects two hearts even when no words are spoken. Love is the courage to be vulnerable, the strength to stay gentle in a harsh world, and the wisdom to choose kindness over ego. It is not about possession, but about presence; not about losing yourself in another, but about finding more of yourself because of them.

Love is not about perfection.

You may hear stories of fairytales where love is flawless, where there are no struggles, no pain, only happiness. But in real life, love is not always like that. True love is not about finding someone perfect—it is about finding someone who sees your imperfections, your scars, your mistakes, and still chooses you, again and again, without hesitation.

Love is freedom, not possession.

If someone truly loves you, they will never try to cage your spirit or silence your voice. They will not dim your light so they can shine brighter. Instead, they will walk beside you, hand in hand, encouraging you to be more of yourself, to grow, to dream, and to live fully. Love is never about control; it is always about respect and trust.

Love is gentle strength.

It is the patience to listen, even when you disagree. It is the kindness to forgive, even when you feel hurt. It is the courage to stay when life becomes hard, and the wisdom to let go when holding on would destroy you.

Love is in the little things.

It is in the hand that reaches for yours when you are tired. It is in the voice that says, *"I believe in you"* when you doubt yourself. It is in the silence where you feel safe, in the laughter that feels like home, and in the tears that are wiped away with care.

When love comes, you will feel it—not only in your heart but in your soul. It will not feel like a storm that shakes you, but like a steady flame that warms you. It will not confuse you; it will bring clarity. It will not hurt your soul; it will nurture it. And even if heartbreak crosses your path, may it only teach you lessons, never take away your belief in love. For the greatest truth is this: **love is not meant to break you, love is meant to make you whole.**

When I speak of love, I speak from my own journey. Love came to me not as a perfect fairytale, but as a mix of joy, struggle, and strength. I found love in someone who saw me beyond my flaws, who made me laugh on heavy days and gave me peace when silence spoke louder than words. It was not always easy.

There were doubts, tears, and battles that tested my faith in what we had. Yet, I learned that true love is not measured by how smooth the path is, but by the choice to stand together through storms.

This love taught me patience, forgiveness, and the difference between attachment and truth. It showed me that real love doesn't chain you—it frees you, nurtures you, and helps you grow. So, remember, my girl, love is not always easy, but when it is real, it is worth every struggle.

Love, for me, has been both a blessing and a test. I have known the butterflies in my stomach, the smiles that come without reason, and the comfort of being seen by someone who feels like home. But I have also known the ache of waiting, the silence of misunderstandings, and the weight of giving my heart where it was not always protected.

Love taught me patience when I wanted quick answers. It taught me forgiveness when my heart was heavy. It showed me how powerful trust is, and how fragile it can become once broken. I have felt love as a safe place, but also as a battlefield where I had to choose between holding on and letting go.

I faced questions, barriers, and battles that tried to shake my belief. There were nights I cried, mornings I doubted, and moments I almost let go. Yet, something deeper always pulled me back—a truth that love is not meant to be easy, it is meant to be real. And perhaps the most beautiful gift love has given me is *you*. For in the warmth of this love, I imagined your smile, your laughter, and your future. He may never know it fully, but his presence gave me the courage to dream of being not just a woman, not just a partner, but also a mother.

Do you know, my dear,

people will tell you that love is nothing but a fairytale. That one day a prince will come on his white horse and take you away, full of love and joy.

This is not the reality of **love**, my dear. love is raw, love is pure, love is hope that helps you survive a nightmare, he will be a human with imperfections and you will have to see the beauty within them. he has to do the same with you, my princess.

When love comes into your life, remember these truths I learned along the way:

- Choose love that makes you feel safe, protected, and respected.
- Do not mistake attention for affection, or control for care.
- Wait for the one who respects your silence as much as your laughter.
- Love should never ask you to shrink yourself to fit someone else's world—it should celebrate the queen that you are.
- And above all, never forget to love yourself first, for only then will you know what you truly deserve.

"These are the compass points for your heart."

One day, you will write your own story of love—different from mine, yet carrying pieces of the wisdom I leave you with. My prayer for you is simple: may you find a love that feels like home, that helps you grow, and that never lets you forget your worth.

Carry these words with you, my darling, and let them guide your heart when the world tries to confuse it. For no matter where life takes you, know this—**you are worthy of a love that is gentle, strong, and everlasting and when love finds you, may it remind you every day that you were always enough.**

With a heart full of love,

Your MUMMA.

ON FRIENDSHIP

My dearest daughter,

One day, you will meet people who call themselves your friend.

And you may then wonder what true friendship really means.

Let me tell you: friendship is not just about laughter, shared secrets, or fun times. True friendship is a bond that survives distance, disagreements, and even mistakes. It is the silent promise that someone will stand by you when life feels heavy, and will celebrate your joys without envy.

Friendship, my dear, is a mirror. A real friend reflects not only your strengths but also your weaknesses in a way that helps you grow. They do not judge you for your flaws or try to change the essence of who you are. They cheer for you when you succeed, comfort you when you fail, and sometimes even say the hard things you need to hear but don't want to.

Friendship is a bond of trust, love, and understanding that connects hearts in a way words often cannot.

It is the safe place where you can be completely yourself, share your joys and sorrows, and find comfort without judgment. True friends celebrate your successes, support you in your struggles, and stand by you even when life becomes difficult.

Friendship is not about how long someone stays, but about the depth of care, loyalty, and honesty shared in the time you have together.

Friendship is like your favorite pair of socks—comfortable, warm, and sometimes a little silly, but always there to make life better.

It's knowing that someone will still like you even when you act a little crazy. True friends are the people who show up with snacks when you're sad, dance with you when you're happy, and stick around through all your ups and downs, no matter how messy life gets.

I have known friendships that felt like home—people with whom I could be completely myself, laugh until my stomach hurt, cry without shame, and share dreams I couldn't tell anyone else.

And I have known friendships that taught me tough lessons—friends who betrayed my trust, walked away in my need, or grew apart. *"They stabbed me in the back like strangers, leaving wounds I never expected."*

Both kinds taught me something vital: that not every friend is meant to stay forever, and that is okay. Real friendship does not demand permanence; it values honesty, depth, and mutual respect in the moments it exists.

Through these experiences, I learned that not all friendships are meant to last, but every friendship teaches a lesson.

Some teach patience, some forgiveness, and some the importance of protecting your heart. Treasure the ones who stay,

"I remember a friend who stayed up all night to listen to me cry—it's memories like these that show the true magic of friendship. who lift you, and who make your tears lighter and your laughter brighter.

There will be friends who test you, who argue with you, who push your patience to its limits. Some will even hurt you unintentionally.

But remember this: true friends are not perfect—they are human. What matters is their heart, their intentions, and their willingness to grow with you. A friend who apologizes, who makes the effort, who celebrates your happiness without jealousy, is worth keeping for a lifetime.

A friend is a **boon** if real:

a blessing in your life who lifts you when you're down, laughs at your silly jokes, keeps your secrets safe, and stands by you even when the world turns away. They are the ones who bring light to your darkest days and make life feel easier, warmer, and sweeter just by being there.

But a friend can be a **bomb** if fake:

a hidden danger that can explode at the wrong moment, leaving heartbreak, betrayal, and lessons you never wanted to learn. Fake friends smile in front of you but gossip behind your back, pretend to care but disappear when you need them, and sometimes even hurt you more than strangers ever could.

So, my sweetheart, choose wisely. Real friends are rare gems that you hold close to your heart. Fake ones? Let them go before they leave a mark. Friendship, when true, is magic. Friendship, when false, is chaos.

So, my dear, when you choose your friends, keep these truths in mind:

- Seek friends who respect your heart, your choices, and your boundaries.
- Distance yourself from those who bring constant negativity, gossip, or jealousy into your life.
- True friendship is reciprocal; it is a bond built on care, trust, and mutual growth.
- Never settle for friends who make you feel small; the right friends will lift you, inspire you, and make you feel seen.
- Celebrate your friends' successes as if they were your own, and forgive them for their mistakes as you hope to be forgiven.

Remember, friendship is not about how many people call themselves your friends – it is about a few souls who truly stand by you, no matter what. They are your pillars in stormy times, your laughter in quiet moments, and often, your family by choice.

I want you to be the kind of friend who makes others feel safe, loved, and celebrated. But also, I want you to protect your own heart. Invest your love and trust wisely. Some people are meant to stay for life; others are meant to teach you lessons. Both are gifts, and both are necessary.

May you always find friends who are loyal, kind, and true. May your heart recognize the ones who are meant to stay, and may you never settle for anything less than respect, trust, and warmth. Because my dear, you are the queen of your own heart.

With all my love,
Your Mumma.

ON STRENGTH AND RESILIENCE

My dearest daughter,

There is something I want you to carry in your heart always: life is not a straight path. It will twist, turn, and sometimes feel impossibly heavy. But within you lies a power far greater than any obstacle—the power of **strength** and the gift of **resilience**.

What is Strength?

Strength is often mistaken for being unbreakable, but real strength is far more subtle and beautiful. It is the quiet voice inside you that whispers, *"You can keep going,"* even when fear and doubt roar around you.

Strength is not just about physical power; it is about emotional courage, moral integrity, and the ability to hold your heart together when everything seems to fall apart.

It is strength that allows you to forgive when it is easier to hate, to love when it is easier to withdraw, and to keep dreaming when the world tells you to give up.

What is Resilience?

Resilience is the art of bouncing back. It is the skill of taking life's punches and using them to grow stronger, wiser, and braver.

Life will test you—sometimes gently, sometimes mercilessly—but resilience is what helps you rise after every fall. It is not about avoiding pain or never failing; it is about **embracing failure as a teacher**, learning from your mistakes, and knowing that setbacks are not the end of the road—they are the stepping stones toward your growth.

Let me share something from my own life, so you can understand these words not as lessons, but as experiences I have lived:

There were moments when I felt completely overwhelmed, when challenges seemed too heavy for my shoulders. But I learned that strength is found in small choices—choosing to smile, to keep going, to help someone even when my heart was tired.

I learned that resilience grows when you refuse to let fear dictate your decisions, when you rise after every failure, and when you remind yourself that your worth is never defined by someone else's opinion.

I want you to understand that life may sometimes push you to the edge, but the human spirit is capable of miracles.

You may stumble, you may cry, and you may even want to give up—but those are the moments when your strength and resilience are forming, like diamonds created **under pressure.**

So, my darling daughter, when you feel shattered, remember this:

- **Believe in yourself**—even when the world doubts you, trust your instincts and your heart.

- **Face challenges bravely**—avoidance may feel safe, but courage grows when you confront what scares you.
- **Learn from mistakes**—each mistake carries a lesson that will make you stronger and wiser.
- **Take care of your mind and body**—strength is holistic; a healthy mind and body give you the energy to endure.
- **Practice gratitude and hope**—even in hard times, find small joys and cling to the belief that tomorrow can be better.

"Here are a few life lessons your Mumma wishes she had learned in her childhood, but doesn't want you to miss:"

- Strength is gentle, not aggressive. It is patience, persistence, and the ability to rise with grace.
- Resilience is forgiving yourself for mistakes and finding courage in the cracks of your heart.
- Challenges are not punishments—they are opportunities to discover who you truly are.
- Your struggles will one day become your wisdom, and your pain will become your power.
- No matter what happens, you are never alone. My love is with you, always.

My beloved daughter, as you read these words, I hope you remember this:

you are capable of enduring, of rising, and of shining brighter than the storms around you.

Life may judge you, but you are stronger than you know, braver than you believe, and more resilient than any challenge you face.

Keep these lessons close, practice them daily, and *remember that falling does not mean failing,* but if you fail you can rise again so my dear rise like the brightest sun after that gloomy weather.

Strength and resilience are not just words – they are a way of life, a compass that will guide you through storms, a light that will illuminate the darkest paths. Hold them in your heart, nurture them, and let them shape you into the magnificent woman I know you will become.

With my full heart

Your Mumma.

ON DREAMS AND AMBITION

My dearest daughter,

There's something I want you to always remember, something etched so deep in my heart that I can't keep it inside. Life will offer you many roads, and sudden turns, and sometimes it won't give you a choice—it will just push you where it wants to. But in all of this, you must never lose sight of your dream. A dream is not a pretty picture in your head; it is your light, your compass, your reason to wake up even on the darkest days.

When I was your age, I had big, wild dreams: to travel, to write, to see the world in colours I had never imagined. But somewhere between responsibilities, expectations, and fear, I folded those dreams and placed them in a box. I thought I could open it later. But life has a strange way of keeping you busy—you get caught up, and soon enough, later never comes.

That's why I'm telling you this today. Don't wait. Don't shrink yourself just because the world says your dreams are too big. Don't let the voices outside be louder than the voice inside your heart.

Darling, ambition is not selfishness. Wanting to reach somewhere is not arrogance. Never let anyone make you feel guilty for wanting more. I have seen how people try to tame a girl's fire, to convince her that comfort is enough, that she should settle for less than she deserves. They will tell you to be satisfied, to stay small, to not shine too brightly. But my love, you were not born to be dim.

You know, dreams are delicate things—they get hurt easily. People may laugh at you. They may say, "This is not possible." And sometimes, even you will doubt yourself. That is the hardest part—the days when you look at yourself in the mirror and wonder if you are enough. I want you to know, in those moments, that you are more than enough. The blood that runs in you, the courage you carry, is stronger than you think.

Let me tell you something I learned too late: your ambition will scare people, because it reminds them of the risks they never took. But that is not your burden to carry. Walk your path with grace, but also with fire. Don't apologize for having a dream so big it shakes your bones.

My darling, there will be sacrifices. To hold onto a dream, you might lose people, comfort, sleep, and sometimes even love. Ambition can be lonely. But that loneliness will build you, shape you, make you powerful. Every sleepless night, every tear, every "no" you hear, will become part of your strength. You will learn to rise, even when you're tired of falling.

And when you do rise, oh daughter, it will be beautiful. It will not just be your victory; it will be mine too. Because in you, I see the second chance I never had. Don't get me wrong—I don't want you to live *my* dreams. I want you to live *yours.* But I want you to live them fully, boldly, with no fear of judgment.

You might fail sometimes. In fact, I want you to. Failure is not an enemy; it is a teacher. I have failed more times than I can count. And yet, "Every failure carved me—softening some parts and hardening others." Don't hide from failure, my child. Embrace it. Let it bruise you, and then let it heal you. Only then will you know the sweetness of true success.

My dear, dreams and ambition are not separate things. A dream is the seed, but ambition is the water and sunlight. Without ambition, dreams stay asleep, and without dreams, ambition has nowhere to go. Keep both alive. Let them feed each other. Let them carry you forward.

One day, when you look back, I want you to say, "I tried. I lived. I didn't stay caged." That's all that matters. Not the awards, not the money, not even what people will say. What matters is that you honoured your soul. That you didn't betray the little girl inside you who once imagined a life full of colours.

And promise me this—when you succeed, don't forget where you came from. Don't forget humility. Ambition should never kill kindness. Be strong, but also gentle. Be fierce, but also compassionate. Let your success never turn into pride so heavy that you can't bow your head in gratitude.

Sometimes, you will feel torn between choosing what the heart wants and what the world wants from you. In those moments, close your eyes and listen quietly. The heart always whispers, while the world shouts. It will take courage to choose that whisper over the noise. But I believe in your courage. I always have.

My daughter, I am not just giving you advice—I am giving you, my truth. My story. The raw parts of me that still ache for the things I left undone. I don't want you to live in regret.

I don't want you to sit at sixty, looking out of a window, thinking, "What if?"

So, go. Chase your dream with both hands. Run after it until your lungs burn. And when you get tired, rest if you must, but never quit. Life will test you, push you to your limits, make you doubt yourself. But remember this: you carry not only your own dream but also the unspoken dreams of all the women before you who never had the chance.

And when you win: win loudly. Win proudly. Win for yourself, but also win for me, for your grandmother, for every woman who was told to stay small. Win because you were born to.

I love you beyond words. And no matter where you go, no matter how far your dreams take you, I will always be here—rooting for you, proud of you, and whispering in your ear: *My child. Fly without fear.*

Forever yours,
Mom

ON HEARTBREAK AND HEALING

My precious daughter,

One day, whether you want it or not, your heart will break. I wish I could shield you from it, hold you in my arms forever so no pain ever touches you—but life doesn't work that way. Love doesn't work that way.

The same heart that teaches you to laugh until your stomach hurts will one day teach you how to ache until you cannot breathe. And as your mother, I cannot stop that storm from coming. All I can do is tell you how to walk through it.

Heartbreak is not just about losing a person. Sometimes it is about losing a dream, a friendship, or a future you thought was certain. It can come from betrayal, from silence, from distance, or simply from time. The person you once loved most can become a stranger you barely recognize. That is what makes heartbreak so cruel—it doesn't just hurt; it shocks you.

The first time it happens, it may feel like your world has ended. You may lie in bed staring at the ceiling, wondering how everything you built with someone could collapse overnight. You will feel hollow, as if your heart is bleeding without a wound. And you will whisper to yourself, *"I will never survive this."*

But you will.

I know you will, because I did. Heartbreak bent me so badly I thought I would never stand again. I cried into pillows until they were drenched. I walked through days wearing a smile while inside I was in pieces. And then came the night when I promised myself: *This will not destroy me.*

And it didn't.

My daughter, heartbreak is not the end. It is the beginning of truly knowing yourself. The one who leaves you does not take your worth with them. They cannot decide whether you are enough. Their absence does not make you less. Their silence does not erase your voice.

When the pain is fresh, you may want to run back, to beg, to ask, *"Why wasn't I enough?"* Don't. If someone cannot see your value, that blindness belongs to them, not to you. Love should never demand that you shrink yourself just to fit in someone else's story.

Healing, though, is never quick. It is slow, messy, frustrating. Some days you will feel free, and the next morning a song, a place, or a scent will drag you back into the ache. That is normal. Healing is not a straight road—it is a river that bends, sometimes rushing, sometimes barely moving. Be patient with yourself. Don't punish yourself for still hurting.

Cry when you must, my love. Tears are not weakness; they are the saltwater that cleanses the wound. Write down your feelings. Pour them into a diary. Talk to me, to yourself, even to the sky. Do not bury it—buried pain turns into poison.

And while you heal, come back to yourself. Love has a way of making us forget who we are. We give so much of ourselves to another that when they leave, we feel empty. But you are not empty—you are whole. Pick up the hobbies you set aside, the dreams you postponed, the colours you once loved. Rebuild your world around you.

Do not rush into new love just to cover the old wound. A broken heart cannot be patched by another person; it must be stitched by your own hands. And when you have healed, love will find you again. When it does, you will love differently—wiser, braver, deeper.

I must tell you something you may not like: your heart may break more than once. That is life. But every time, you will also grow stronger. You will discover new versions of yourself. And one day, you will realize heartbreak was not a punishment—it was a teacher. It taught you what you deserve and what you must never settle for again.

Promise me this: never let heartbreak harden you. Don't close your doors out of fear. Don't let one wrong person convince you that love isn't real. Love is real. I see it in the way you laugh, in the way you care, in the way you dream. Your heart is too precious to live in fear. Let the pain teach you, but not define you.

Healing is not forgetting. It is remembering without bleeding. One day, you will look back and say, *"Yes, it hurt me, but it also built me."* The memory of the one who hurt you will stop feeling like a knife and start feeling like a story—just a chapter, not your whole book.

And then you will find peace. You will wake up one morning and realize your heart no longer aches. The sun will shine the same, but this time you will feel it shining for you. You will smile again—not the forced smile, but the one that lights up your eyes.

That day you will know: heartbreak did not end you. It gave birth to a stronger, braver, wiser version of you.

My darling, heartbreak will change you, but it does not have to break you forever. Healing will shape you, but it does not have to erase your softness. Carry both—the scar and the strength, the pain and the lesson. That is how you become whole again.

So, when the day comes, when you feel broken, remember my words. Remember your mother once walked through the same fire and survived. Remember that no matter how shattered you feel, you are never alone—I will always be here.

And when the healing has done its quiet work, I hope you love again. Love with the same courage, the same tenderness, the same wild heart. Because no matter how many times it breaks, love is always worth it.

With all my love,

Your Mumma

ON SELF-WORTH

My precious girl,

Come, sit close to me. I don't want you to just hear these words; I want you to feel them in your bones. I want them to live inside you like a second heartbeat. Because this lesson, my love, is not from books, not from schools, not from the world—it is from me, your mother, who has watched you breathe, fall, rise, and shine since the day you were born. This is about your self-worth.

Do you remember, my child, how you used to come running to me after school, your little hands clutching a report card? Some days, your face glowed, other days your eyes welled up.

And every time you looked at me, waiting, almost trembling, I saw the question in your eyes: *"Am I enough, Maa?"*

That question breaks my heart. Because, my love, your worth is not written on a piece of paper. Not in grades. Not in trophies. Not in medals. Not in the claps of teachers or the praise of friends. Your worth is older than all of that. It was etched into your soul the moment you were born.

I still remember holding you as a newborn, so tiny, so fragile. You didn't have straight A's, you didn't have perfect hair, you didn't have followers or likes—you only had a heartbeat. And that heartbeat was worth more than anything in this universe. That heartbeat made you enough then, and it makes you enough now. Nothing can take that away.

But let me tell you the truth, and this part will sting: sometimes you are your own enemy.

Yes, you, my daughter. I've seen you apologize for existing. I've seen you say "sorry" when you had nothing to be sorry for. I've seen you bend, shrink, twist yourself into smaller and smaller versions just to fit into places too small for your soul. And every time I watch you do that, I feel both pain and anger.

I want to grab your shoulders and shake you. I want to shout, *"Stop doing that to yourself! You are not a burden, you are not 'too much,' you are not unworthy."* Do you hear me? Stop giving discounts on your worth. Stop handing over your crown for free. Stop lowering your voice so others can feel louder.

Because here is the truth—if you do not value yourself, no one else will. If you do not set the standard, the world will treat you however it pleases. And beta, I refuse to watch my child become a doormat for a world that has already forgotten how precious she is.

There will be days—yes, I know this—when life will crush you. When someone leaves you, betrays you, hurts you; when you will fail, when you will stumble, when you will question everything. On those days, the cruel voice inside your head will whisper, *"See? You're not enough. You don't matter."*

On those days, I want you to remember this: you are not your mistakes. You are not your heartbreaks. You are not your failures. You are the courage with which you rise again. You are the compassion with which you still love. And the fire inside you refuse to burn out, no matter how many storms try to drown you.

Self-worth doesn't come from being perfect. It comes from knowing that even when you are broken, even when you are tired, even when you are misunderstood—you are still enough.

Let me tell you something else. Sometimes, my child, I get angry with you. Angry because I see you chasing after people who don't even deserve a place in your shadow. Angry because you cry over those who wouldn't even notice if you disappeared. Angry because you lower your standards, your dignity, just to feel loved.

And then I stop, I breathe. I realize my anger is love in disguise. It is not anger at you, but anger at the world that makes you doubt yourself. My love for you is too fierce, too wild, too unshakable to ever sit quietly while you treat yourself as less.

So, if I sound harsh, if my words burn, remember this: they are fire to keep you warm, not fire to hurt you. I will scold you when you forget your worth, but I will also hold you close when you cannot remember how to love yourself. Because that is what mothers do.

And listen carefully now, because this is the promise I want from you:

- Never shrink yourself just to make others comfortable.
- Never silence your voice because the room is too loud.
- Never run after those who walk away from you.

- Never beg anyone to see your value—it shines whether they notice or not.

These are the rules of your heart.

Follow them always.

Promise me you will protect your heart, your dignity, your dreams. Promise me that even when you fall, you will rise without doubting that you belong here. Promise me that when you look into the mirror, you will not search for flaws, but for the miracle that I see every time I look at you.

Because that's who you are—a miracle.

One last thing, my precious girl. I know there will be moments when my words will fade, when my voice will be far away, when the silence of the world will drown you. But even then, remember this: *your mother believes in you.* Always.

Unconditionally. I have carried your worth inside me since before you could breathe, and if you ever forget it, I will hold it safe until you remember again.

You are enough. You are worthy. You are priceless.

And no matter where life takes you, no matter how the world tries to measure you, you will always be my miracle.

With all my love, and even the love I haven't yet learned to express.
your MUMMA

ON SPIRITUALITY AND VALUES

My dearest child,

Today I don't want to speak to you like a teacher or guide, but as a mother whose heart overflows with faith and love. What I am about to tell you is not just advice, but the very truth that has carried me through nights of tears and days of joy. I want to talk to you about spirituality and values – about the invisible roots that hold us steady, and the eternal hands of God that never let us fall.

Spirituality, my love, is not about rules alone. It is not about counting beads without feeling, or bowing your head without devotion. True spirituality is about recognizing that behind every moment – behind the sunrise, behind your breath, behind the smallest smile – there is God. And God is not far away. God is within you, around you, and above you, always listening, always watching, always holding you.

When you whisper "Om Namah Parvati Pataye, Har Har Mahadev", you are not just calling Shiva, you are calling the destroyer of your fears, the one who breaks illusions and shows you truth.

When you fold your hands to Ganesh ji, you are not just bowing to an idol, but asking the remover of obstacles to clear your path, to bless your beginnings, to hold your hand when life feels heavy.

When you pray to Saraswati Maa, you invite wisdom into your heart – not just knowledge of books, but the wisdom to know right from wrong, the wisdom to live with purity.

Never forget, my child: Durga Maa lives inside you. Her strength, her fierceness, her unstoppable energy – it flows in your veins. When the world tries to push you down, remember her. Call her name. She will rise inside you.

And when fear grips you, whisper to Kali Maa, for she is the destroyer of darkness. She will remind you that no demon – whether outside you or inside your mind – is stronger than the fire of the Divine Mother.

And when life feels too heavy to carry, when your shoulders ache with burdens, remember Hanuman ji. Remember his courage, his loyalty, his strength. Say his name – "Jai Bajrang Bali!" – and feel the chains of fear shatter. When you think you are small, when you think you are weak, remember that Hanuman carried mountains in his hands. His strength is also your strength.

My dear one, values are also worship. To live with truth is to honour Ram ji, who lived a life of dharma even when it cost him everything.

To live with devotion is to honour Krishna ji and Radha Rani, whose love was not bound by the world's rules but flowed like music – eternal, pure, divine.

To live with courage is to honour the Goddess, who slayed demons not for glory but to protect the innocent.

To live with compassion is to honour Shiva, who drank poison so that the world could survive.

Do you see, my child? Values are not just rules – they are how you live God in your daily life. Every time you speak the truth when it is hard, you are bowing to Ram ji. Every time you forgive instead of hate, you are honouring Krishna ji. Every time you learn with humility, you are touching the feet of Saraswati Maa. Every time you rise after being broken, you are carrying Durga Maa inside your chest. Every time you act with courage despite trembling, you are walking with Hanuman ji.

Spirituality without values is empty – it is like chanting without devotion, or fire without warmth. And values without spirituality can become rigid – rules followed without heart. But when the two come together, my child, your life becomes worship. Every breath becomes a mantra. Every step becomes a prayer.

Life will test you. People will mock your faith. They will say God is not real, or that values are outdated. They will tell you that success comes from money, not honesty. They will tempt you to cheat, to lie, to break promises.

And in those moments, I want you to close your eyes and hear the chant that has saved generations:

"Om Namah Shivaya.

Om Dum Durgaayei Namah.

Jai Hanuman Gyan Gun Sagar.

Jai Shri Ram.

Radhe Radhe Govinda."

These are not just words, my child. These are shields. They are swords. They are rivers of strength flowing through your veins. Say them with your heart, and no force on earth can break you.

Values will guide you when your heart is confused. When the world tells you to take shortcuts, honesty will whisper, "No, my child, stand tall." When anger tells you to hurt someone, kindness will whisper, "No, my child, rise above." When fear tells you to hide, courage will whisper, "No, my child, speak the truth."

Do not think values make you weak. They make you powerful in ways the world does not understand. To be honest when others lie, to be kind when others are cruel, to forgive when others seek revenge – this is not weakness. This is strength. This is dharma. This is God moving through you.

And when you doubt yourself, remember the stories. Remember Ram ji walking through exile with dignity. Remember Sita Maa's unshakable purity. Remember Krishna's laughter in the darkest of wars. Remember Radha's endless love. Remember Hanuman's devotion. Remember Shiva's stillness. Remember Parvati Maa's patience. Remember Durga Maa's power. Remember Kali Maa's fire. Remember Saraswati Maa's wisdom. All of them live inside you. You are never alone.

My sweet child, spirituality and values are not about perfection. You will fall. You will stumble. You will make mistakes. But each time you rise with truth, each time you return to God, you are stronger than before. My child, the world will change, people will disappoint, and life will be unpredictable. But spirituality and values will remain your anchor. They will be your sanctuary, your guide, and your strength. Live with them in your heart, carry them in your actions, and share them in your words. And remember, I am with you in spirit, always. Even when I cannot speak these words aloud, even when distance separates us, know that my love and guidance are woven into your very being.

Cherish the sacred. Cherish your values. Let them shape your life, guide your choices, and fill your heart. And know this, my dear: a life lived with spirituality and values, even quietly, is a life that shines brighter than any spotlight the world could ever offer.

With all the faith in my soul, with every prayer on my lips, with the blessings of Mahadev and Maa Shakti upon you always.

Your MUMMA

ON WOMANHOOD AND FEMININITY

My beloved daughter,

Come sit with me for a moment. Don't rush, don't look away—just be here. I want these words to reach not only your ears but the deepest corners of your heart. Today, I want to talk to you about something that has been misunderstood, twisted, celebrated, and sometimes even shamed by the world. Something sacred. Something powerful. Something that belongs to you, and only you.

I want to talk to you about womanhood. About femininity. About the soul of who you are.

Being a woman, my darling, has nothing to do with wearing the "right" dress, painting your face a certain way, or walking a certain walk that others approve of. Womanhood cannot be stitched into fabric or hidden in rules written by someone else. It is not a script you must memorize; it is a song that lives in your blood. A song only you can sing.

It is about embracing yourself completely—the storm and the calm, the fire and the tenderness, the warrior and the healer. You are not meant to be cut into halves. You are not "too much" of anything. You are whole, exactly as you are.

Never—never—let anyone make you feel that being feminine is weakness. That is one of the greatest lies the world has told women. Your femininity is not fragile porcelain to be kept on a shelf. It is steel wrapped in silk. It is wisdom hidden in gentleness. It is love that heals and fire that burnt at the same time.

Femininity is not small—it is vast. It stretches beyond labels, beyond boundaries. To be feminine is to cry when your heart aches and still rise the next morning. To be feminine is to bleed every month and still create life out of that body. To be feminine is to forgive when you could destroy, to nurture when you could abandon, to create when you could break.

But, my love, being a woman will not always be easy. The world will test you. There will be times when your voice will be silenced, when your choices will be questioned, when your very existence will be weighed and measured by people who do not even know your soul. You will be judged for being too ambitious, too loud, too quiet, too bold, too emotional—too much of everything and never enough of anything.

But here is what I need you to remember: **your womanhood is not theirs to define.** It belongs only to you. The way you live it, the way you honour it—that is your truth, your shield, your strength.

Your femininity is not a weakness to hide; it is an art to master. It is your magic, your power, your secret weapon. It is in the way you laugh until your eyes water, the way you notice the details others miss, the way you hold someone's hand and make them feel seen, the way you stand tall when life wants to break you down.

Don't ever apologize for feeling deeply. For crying in the middle of the night, for caring too much, for loving without holding back. Sensitivity is not a flaw—it is a gift. Intuition is not foolishness—it is wisdom the world has forgotten.

And remember this: ambition and femininity are not enemies. Do not let anyone fool you into believing that to dream big you must become hard, or that to care you must remain small. You can be fierce and gentle. You can lead armies and still cradle a child. You can run after your dreams and still love with a soft heart. Your femininity does not shrink your strength—it expands it.

My daughter, your womanhood also means claiming your body and mind as sacred ground. This body you live in—it is not shameful. It is not dirty. It is a temple. Every curve, every scar, every mark tells a story. Honour it. Protect it. Love it.

And your mind—ah, your mind—is your greatest weapon and your safest home. Fill it with knowledge, protect it from poison, and let it bloom. Do not let anyone tell you that your worth lies only in your face or your body. You are valuable simply because you exist, because your soul breathes in this world.

Being a woman also means knowing the power of sisterhood. Never look at another woman as your competition. Look at her as your reflection, your ally, your sister. We rise higher when we rise together. If you ever see another woman being diminished, stand beside her, not above her. Because true womanhood is not about comparison—it is about connection. Together, we break walls. Together, we rewrite stories. Together, we make this world safer for the daughters yet to come.

There will be days when you doubt yourself, when the mirror feels cruel, when the voices of the world make you question your beauty, your intelligence, your worth. On those days, I want you to close your eyes and remember this: **you are not**

fragile. You are not small. You are a storm disguised as a sunrise. You are an ocean contained in human form.

Do not shrink to make others comfortable. Do not dim your brilliance to fit into darkness. Do not apologize for existing loudly, boldly, beautifully.

Celebrate yourself. Celebrate your body as it changes, your heart as it loves and breaks, your mind as it learns, your soul as it grows. Celebrate the scars, because they mean you healed. Celebrate the tears, because they mean you cared. Celebrate your sensuality, your strength, your softness, your rage. Celebrate every cycle, every stage, every transformation. This is your birthright. This is the power of being a woman.

And finally, my darling, carry this truth forever: **womanhood is sacred, and so are you.** Walk this earth with your head held high. Speak your truth, even when your voice shakes. Love with your whole heart, even when it hurts. Be kind, even when it's easier to be cruel. The world may not always understand you—but you do not need its permission to exist as you are.

So, hold these words close, like a prayer, like armour:

- You are strong, even when you feel fragile.
- You are beautiful, even when the world cannot see it.
- You are powerful, even when they try to break you.
- You are enough—always, endlessly, simply because you are.

And I promise you this: I will always be here. Believing in you. Protecting you. Loving you. Because you, my daughter, are extraordinary.

You are a living miracle. You are proof of the sacred power of womanhood. And the world is lucky—so very lucky—to witness your light.

With all my love and awe,
Mumma

ON COURAGE TO BE DIFFERENT

My dearest daughter,

From the very first moment I held you in my arms, I knew the world would try to shape you in ways that don't belong to you. People will tell you how to look, how to act, how to dream, and even how to feel. Sometimes, they will not even realize they are trying to Mold you, but their words, their expectations, and their fear of what is different will press against your spirit like invisible chains.

I want you to know something very important: it is okay to be different. In fact, it is not just okay—it is necessary. The world does not need another version of someone else. It needs *you*, with your own thoughts, your own laughter, your own heartbreaks, your own triumphs. It needs your curiosity that never settles, your imagination that refuses limits, your heart that feels too much and too deeply.

Being different is not always easy. You will stand out in ways that make others uncomfortable. You will be asked questions, judged quietly, and maybe even laughed at. Some days, you will feel like you are walking alone, carrying your uniqueness like a secret weight. But I promise you this: every time you choose to be yourself, you are lighting a spark that cannot be dimmed. And that spark will not only guide your own path—it will quietly show others that it is possible to be brave too.

You see, courage is not the absence of fear. It is feeling the fear so clearly that your hands shake and your stomach tightens—and still, taking that step forward anyway. It is choosing your own melody in a world full of echoes. It is deciding, quietly and firmly, that you will honour your heart even when it doesn't match what everyone else thinks are "normal" or "right."

I want you to understand that being different is not about rebelling against the world. It is about being faithful to yourself. It is about listening to your own voice, even if it is soft, even if it trembles, even if it sounds strange. That voice inside you—the one that tells you to paint your life with colours no one else has seen, to write your own rules, to love freely and fully—is sacred. Protect it. Trust it. Follow it.

When you choose to be different, you will meet people who do not understand you. Some will call you stubborn, awkward, or strange. Some may try to pull you back into the "safe" path. But remember this: the most remarkable people in history, the ones who changed the world, the ones who created art that made hearts ache and minds expand, were always a little different. They were brave enough to embrace that difference. And so can you.

Do not ever apologize for being who you are. Do not shrink yourself to make others comfortable. Do not dim your light to avoid standing out. Instead, wear your uniqueness like a crown. Let your quirks, your passions, your dreams, your fears, your laughter, your tears—they all belong to the masterpiece that is you. That masterpiece is only complete when you allow every part of yourself to exist freely.

I know it may feel lonely at times. The world may not always celebrate your differences. But in those quiet moments, remember that you are planting seeds. Your courage, your authenticity, your choice to stand apart—it will inspire others, even if you cannot see it. And most importantly, it will bring you closer to yourself, to the life that is meant for you, not the life someone else designed for you.

A small memory I carry: once, when I was young, I wanted to wear a bright scarf to a family gathering. Everyone else favored plain colors. I felt the glance and the whisper, and for a moment my hand hovered near the scarf and then dropped. I almost put it away. But something inside me tightened — a small, stubborn flame — and I wrapped it around my neck. For the first hour I felt every hush like a weight. By the second hour, a cousin asked where I'd bought it, and the woman next to me smiled and said she loved my courage. That small choice to keep the scarf became a quiet lesson: one small act of being myself changed the tone of the room. That is how bravery often begins — not with roars, but with small, steady thorns of truth.

So, my love, be brave. Be wild. Be strange. Be delicate and strong at the same time. Dare to dream in ways that scare you. Dare to love in ways that the world cannot measure. Dare to stand alone when it is needed, knowing that every step you take in truth is worth more than a lifetime of fitting in.

If you ever feel unsure how to begin, try these small practices. They will help you build courage step by gentle step:

- Speak one small truth each day — a preference, an opinion, a "no." Notice how your voice grows steadier.

- Keep a "difference" journal – record moments when you followed your own path, however small. Revisit it when you doubt yourself.
- Find one person who sees you. It could be a friend, an aunt, a teacher. Tell them your small fears; keep each other company.
- Celebrate the tiny rebellions – the red ribbon, the odd book choice, the idea you voiced. Each tiny rebellion is a brick in your own house of courage.

The world may try to ask you to be ordinary. I ask you to be extraordinary. Not for fame, not for recognition, not for applause—but because living as your true self is the only way to live fully. The only way to experience joy, wonder, love, and freedom in its purest form.

And whenever you doubt yourself, remember this: I believe in you. I believe in your fire, your light, your heart, and your mind. I believe in every unique thing that makes you, *you*. And even if the world does not understand your brilliance, I do. I see you. I honour you. I love you exactly as you are—and I always will.

So, step into the world with courage, my darling. Step forward with the quiet power of knowing that your difference is your gift. Step forward knowing that being true to yourself is the greatest act of bravery you will ever perform.

And always remember: the only person you must ever try to be like is you.

With tons of love,

Your Mumma.

ON LEGACY AND FAMILY

My dearest daughter,

There is something I must tell you—something heavy, something that has lived in my bones and heart for as long as I can remember. I carry it quietly, tucked between my ribs, in the spaces where words cannot reach. I carry it because I want you to know, and yet, I want you to be spared. I want you to be free.

Life has not been gentle with me. I have walked through storms that felt endless, nights that swallowed me whole, days where the sun rose but warmth never touched me. I have known hunger—not just of food, but of love, of understanding, of safety. I have been forced to stand in rooms full of people and smile, even when my heart was bleeding, even when I wanted to scream. I have made sacrifices you cannot imagine, worn masks that weighed me down, and swallowed my own dreams so that others could feel at ease.

And I never want you to live that way.

My love, family is not just about blood—it is about love that protects, about hearts that see you even when you hide, about hands that lift you when the world pushes you down. I have seen the kind of suffering that leaves scars unseen, and I am writing these words into your soul so you can understand the weight I carry—and so that you never have to carry it yourself.

Every wrinkle on my hands, every sleepless night, every tear I swallowed silently—they are all part of a story I want you to inherit, not as a burden, but as a shield. I want you to know that even in the moments when life felt cruel, even when the nights were long and empty, I survived. I survived not for myself, but for you.

I want you to know that every struggle I endured, every night I cried into my pillow, every heartbreak I masked with a smile—was for you. For the life I hope you will have. I fought battles so that your hands would never tremble with fear. I bore pain so that you could dance in the sunlight without hesitation. I silenced my own heartbreaks so that your laughter would echo freely, unbroken.

You must understand something, my love: legacy is not in wealth, in houses, in gold. Legacy is in love, in resilience, in courage, in the courage to be kind even when the world is cruel. It is in the lessons passed silently; in the strength we inherit not through instructions but through example. And my dearest, I want my legacy to be a shield for you, a light that never flickers, a map for the times you feel lost.

There will be moments when the world will try to bend you, when it will try to make you small, when it will ask you to choose comfort over truth. And in those moments, I want you to remember my voice inside your heart. I want you to feel the warmth of my arms even when I cannot be there. I want you to know that you are never truly alone because my love surrounds you, it lives in you, it flows through you.

I will tell you secrets I have never told anyone, because you deserve to know the truth of what I carried alone for so long. I have loved people who did not love me back. I have given my everything to those who could not see me. I have endured heartbreaks that nearly broke me, yet I stood. Not because I wanted to survive—I stood because I wanted to live fully, so that one day, I could guide you to do the same.

And you, my darling, will not suffer the way I did. You will stumble, you will hurt, you will feel the sharp edges of life—and that is inevitable—but you will do it with my lessons etched in your soul. You will rise, always. You will rise not because life will be easy, but because you will know that love and family are your true fortress. You will know that even in the darkest moments, someone stood before you and paved the way with courage, with tears, and with relentless hope.

I want you to understand that suffering is not a curse—it is a teacher. But suffering alone, in silence, is a burden I do not wish for you. I want you to cry, yes—but also to be held. I want you to fight, yes—but also to rest. I want you to feel deeply, love completely, and live fiercely, without the fear that your strength will not be enough. Because my love will always be enough. Because our family's legacy is enough.

Family, my love, is the story we write together. It is in the sacrifices, in the laughter, in the silences shared, in the hands held tightly through storms. And the legacy I leave you is this: never be afraid to love fully, never be afraid to feel deeply, and never, ever settle for less than you deserve. Protect yourself, honour yourself, and remember that your lineage is not just mine—it is the story of generations who came before us, who survived, who loved, who fought, so that you could be born into a life that is yours to shape.

I want you to promise me something. Promise me that when life tests you, when it pushes and pulls and threatens to break you, you will remember this: that my heart, my life, my struggles—they were all for you. And in every heartbeat of yours, my love will live on. You are my greatest hope, my eternal joy, my miracle. You are the reason I endured, the reason I dreamed, the reason I believed.

So, my love, grow with courage. Love with fearlessness. Live with your heart wide open. Carry our story, but make it your own. And know, always, that no matter where life takes you, my arms, my heart, my love – they are with you. Always.

This is a short lullaby for you my sweetheart;

"And when the night feels too dark,
When the winds of the world feel too harsh,
Close your eyes, my darling,
And feel my heartbeat in yours.

We are a chain of souls unbroken,
A river of love that flows through generations,
You are the bloom I prayed for in the silence,
The miracle I carried through storms unseen.

Live fiercely.
Love boldly."

And remember – our legacy is not in the past,
It is in you, shining brighter than I ever could.

With heavy heart and love

Your Mumma.

MY FINAL WORDS TO YOU

My darling,

If you are reading this, it means you are stepping into the world with your own light, your own story, your own heart. I want you to feel me beside you, even when I am not there. My love has followed you long before your first breath, and it will follow you long after.

There will be days when the world feels heavy, when shadows press against your soul, and when tears fall freely. On those days, close your eyes and remember: every scar you carry, every ache you feel, every quiet struggle—is not a weakness—it is proof that you are alive, that you are brave, that you are becoming.

Carry courage like a necklace, wear kindness like a crown, and let your heart always guide you. There is no map for the life you are meant to live—only your choices, only your love, only your truth. And I know, my love, that you will navigate it beautifully.

I hope you dance in the rain, laugh until your ribs ache, and cry when your heart needs it. I hope you embrace who you are, even when the world does not understand. I hope you love, not carefully, but recklessly, fully, without fear. And I hope you remember, always, that you are never alone—for my heart beats in yours.

Our story is not finished. It is carried in every step you take, every word you speak, every life you touch. And when your own child asks about love, about courage, about family, you will tell them not just my story—but yours, the one you are creating, one brave, beautiful, unstoppable day at a time.

So go, my darling. Live fully. Love fearlessly. Shine fiercely. And know that I am with you—in the wind that brushes your face, in the sunlight that warms your skin, in the quiet that hums in your soul.

Always,
Your Mumma

With love, always.
Our story continues...

A WHISPER OF LOVE

The last words of a mother are not always spoken—they live in the silence, in the spaces between your heartbeats, in the gentle echo of love that never ends.

"Carry the light I left for you,
Even when the world feels dark.
Carry the love that made you,
Even when you feel small.
Carry the courage I breathed into you,
Even when your own heart trembles.
And know, my darling,
In every step, in every dream,
I am there, always."

With all my love,

Your darling MUMMA.